Wild Horse Summer

~ *By* Hope Ryden ~
Illustrated by Paul Casale

Clarion Books / *New York*

Clarion Books
a Houghton Mifflin Company imprint
215 Park Avenue South, New York, NY 10003
Text copyright © 1997 by Hope Ryden
Illustrations copyright © 1997 by Paul Casale
The text is set in 12.5/16.5 Ehrhardt
The illustrations were executed in pencil on paper

Printed in the U.S.A.

Library of Congress Cataloging-in-Publication Data
Ryden, Hope.
Wild horse summer / Hope Ryden.
p.   cm.
Summary: Alison spends her thirteenth summer on a ranch
in Wyoming where she learns to ride a horse and where Kelly, who is blind,
helps her overcome an old fear.
ISBN 0-395-77519-1
[1. Ranch life—Fiction.   2. Blind—Fiction.   3. Physically
handicapped—Fiction.   4. Fear—Fiction.   5. Wild horses—Fiction.
6. Horse—Fiction.]   I. Title.
PZ7.R9589Wi 1997
[Fic]—dc20   96–14221
CIP
AC

VB 10 9 8 7 6 5 4 3 2 1